Pretty Hair

Carylee Carrington

Archway Publishing books may be ordered through booksellers or by contacting:

Archway Publishing
1663 Liberty Drive
Bloomington, IN 47403
www.archwaypublishing.com
1 (888) 242-5904

ISBN: 978-1-4808-8387-1 (sc)
ISBN: 978-1-4808-8386-4 (hc)
ISBN: 978-1-4808-8407-6 (e)

Print information available on the last page.

Archway Publishing rev. date: 10/28/2019

ARCHWAY
PUBLISHING

It was Sophia's first day at her new school. She woke up to the smell of the blueberry pancakes, her mom was making for breakfast in the kitchen. "Mmmm, my favorite," Sophia thought to herself.

Sophia could not wait to go to her new school. When mom came to get her for breakfast, she was all dressed and ready.

"Well, I see someone is excited for her first day of school," said Mom.

"Oh, yes mommy," answered Sophia. "I've got my new dress, my new shoes, and I love my new hairdo." Sophia shook her head from side to side and giggled. She loved hearing the beads in her hair hit together like tiny wind chimes.

Mom had combed Sophia's hair into cornrows, with blue and white beads to match her dress, just as Sophia had asked - - she wanted everything to be perfect, for her first day of school.

As Sophia ate her favorite breakfast of blueberry pancakes, she grinned with excitement. She couldn't wait to get to her new school.

Sophia walked with her mom to meet her new teacher, Mrs. Ross.

Sophia hugged her mom and waved good-bye as Mrs. Ross took her hand, and together, they walked to her new class.

Sophia entered the class and with a bright smile said "Hello!"

She looked around the room, all the little boys and girls had blonde, brown or red hair. Some curly, some straight and silky, but none of the girls had hair like hers. Sophia took her seat,

"Hello, I'm Sophia," she said to the little girl sitting next to her. She had a headband with a pretty pink bow, in her curly red hair.

"Hello, my name is Margaret, but everyone calls me Maggie," the little girl answered.

At recess Sophia and Maggie played together. A little blonde girl came over to Sophia and Maggie.

"Hi, I'm Jenny," she said, introducing herself.

Sophia smiled and replied, "Hello, my name is Sophia." She was delighted to make a new friend and she liked Jenny's hair. Jenny's hair was golden, very silky, and it gleamed like sunrays. Sophia thought Jenny's hair looked like all the girls in the stories she had read. Her hair styled in two pigtails, with pink bows that matched her pink dress.

Sophia stared, admiring Jenny's hair, but the look on Jenny's face was strange. She pointed at Sophia's hair, she almost tried to touch. Jenny looked very puzzled.

"Why does your hair have lines?" she asked. Jenny had never seen anyone with hair styled like Sophia's before.

Shocked at Jenny's remark, Sophia asked, "What do you mean?"

"Your hair, it looks like lines; and why do have beads on the ends?" she asked.

"They are called cornrows," Sophia explained proudly as she shook her head making the beads hit together like wind chimes, "my mommy did it special, just for me."

"Your mother put corn, in your hair?" Jenny gasped, "Oh my, that's so interesting!" Jenny and the other girls giggled and skipped away.

At the end of recess, Jenny ran up to Sophia. "Look Sophia," Jenny shouted, "I have beans in my hair." Jenny had picked string beans from the school garden and placed them at the top of her pigtails. Jenny felt very pleased with herself, but Sophia was sad. Was Jenny poking fun at her hair? She didn't want her new friends to make fun of her.

As Sophia walked home, she began to take the beads out of her hair. They fell to the ground like a trail of breadcrumbs. She arrived home with half of her hair loosed, looking very sad.

Her mother gasped at the sight of her half loosed hair, "Sophia, what happened to your hair?" she asked.

"I don't like cornrows anymore, a little girl, with pretty golden hair made fun of me." Sophia answered sadly.

Sophia's mom knelt down and gave her a big hug. "Don't worry baby, we'll try something else tomorrow," she told Sophia.

The next day, Sophia asked her mom to style her hair into two pigtails, just like Jenny had. Sophia didn't want them to be braided, she wanted them loose like Jenny. Her pigtails made two poofs, one on each side of her head.

As Sophia arrived at school, she saw her new friend Maggie. They raced to meet each other.

"Good-bye Mommy," Sophia yelled back as she disappeared with Maggie through the doors, into the school.

When Jenny saw Sophia, she ran right over to her. "Now, how'd you do that Sophia?" she asked.

"Do what?" Sophia responded.

"Your hair, it's all puffed up like two balloons on the side of your head," answered Jenny.

Jenny poked at Sophia's hair, and made popping sounds, "Pop! Pop!"

"I don't like that," Sophia told Jenny, as she sadly walked away.

"I'm sorry," Jenny said shocked. She hadn't realized that she hurt Sophia's feelings.

A sad Sophia went home again that day.

She opened the door to the kitchen, her mom was busy cooking.

"Mommy, I want my hair straight and silky like Jenny's," she whined. "Mommy, can you make my hair silky?"

"Sophia, what on earth are you talking about?" Her mom knelt down and gave her a big hug, "Sophia, your hair is perfect, just the way it is!"

"But mom," Sophia complained, with tears streaming down her face, "My hair is so different. It's the most different of anyone in my class. Jenny's hair is so silky and pretty. She said my pigtails looked like balloons."

Sophia's mother wiped the tears from her cheeks and said, "Look at you. Your hair is different, and special, and most of all, it is unique. Your tight curls help to hold beautiful styles. Your hair is beautiful, you are beautiful, and you don't need to be like anybody else. I love your hair and you know what else?"

"What mommy?" Sophia asked, still sniffling.

Mom answered, "Your hair is just like mine, natural and full. Tomorrow, I will give you a beautiful style that shows off your natural beauty. Be confident in who you are, my angel, because you are beautiful!"

Sophia was so happy, she jumped into her mother's arms and gave her a big squeeze. "Thank you, Mommy," she squealed.

The next day her mom gave her a brand-new hairstyle. Sophia loved her new hairstyle. As she walked to school with her mom that morning, she admired her hair as she passed her reflection in the shop windows and cars that lined her path. She held her head high, with a confident smile, "I'm going to have a great day," Sophia said to herself, "no matter what anyone says."

As she arrived at school, Sophia saw Jenny with her mother. She started to walk closely behind her mother as Jenny and her mother approached.

"Look mommy, there's Sophia," Jenny said giddily. Jenny ran, pulling her mother along to meet Sophia. "Sophia, Sophia!" Jenny yelled out. "Look mom, it's different again today." Jenny, reached out her hand to touch Sophia's hair, but Sophia hid behind her mother.

Jenny's mother came closer and leaned in to Sophia, "So you're the little girl with the pretty hair? I've heard so much about you."

Sophia peeked out from behind her mother. She looked up at her mother, who smiled and urged her to step forward.

Jenny's eyes gleamed as she gasped to see Sophia, "Wow Sophia, your hair looks like a crown. You're a princess! See mommy, her hair is magic. Mommy can you do my hair like Sophia's?"

"Sorry, Jenny," her mom answered, "I don't think I can."

"I love your hair, Jenny," Sophia spoke up, "Your hair is very pretty. It glows in the sun and it flows in the wind. And you know what's best of all?"

"What?" Jenny asked.

Sophia leaned over and whispered in Jenny's ear, "Your hair is just like your mother's."

"Princess Sophia, with her hair like a crown," Jenny curtsied to Sophia.

"Princess Jenny, with the golden hair," Sophia curtsied to Jenny.

Both girls looked up at their mothers and smiled.

"We both have pretty princess hair," they giggled.

With hugs from their moms, these two new best-friends were ready for school. They both were full of smiles as they ran side by side, up the steps, and through the doors.

Different styles, long or short, curly or straight, red, black, brown, blonde or whatever color or style it may be, your hair is beautiful, naturally.

CPSIA information can be obtained
at www.ICGtesting.com
Printed in the USA
JSHW020535131119
2391JS00002BA/14